British Library Cataloguing in Publication Data

Inkpen, Mick
Threadbear.
I. Title
823.914 [J]

ISBN 0-340-57350-3

Text and illustrations copyright © Mick Inkpen 1990

The right of Mick Inkpen to be identified as the author
of this work has been asserted by him in accordance with
the Copyright, Designs and Patents Act 1988.

First published 1990 by Hodder and Stoughton Children's Books
Picture Knight edition first published 1992
Second impression 1992

Published by Hodder and Stoughton Children's Books,
a division of Hodder and Stoughton Ltd,
Mill Road, Dunton Green, Sevenoaks, Kent TN13 2YA.

Printed in Italy by L.E.G.O., Vicenza

THREADBEAR

MICK INKPEN

**Picture
Knight**

HODDER AND STOUGHTON

Ben's bear was called
Threadbear. He was old.
Bits of him had worn
out. Or worked loose.
Or dropped off.

He had a paw which
didn't match, and a button
for an eye. When he looked
through the button he saw four pictures
instead of one. It was like looking in a
television shop window.

But there was one thing that had always
been wrong with Threadbear. The silly man who
had made him had put too much stuffing inside
him. His arms were too hard. His legs were too
hard. And there was so much stuffing inside his
tummy that his squeaker had been squashed.
It had never squeaked. Not even once.

Threadbear hated having a squeaker in his tummy that wouldn't squeak. It made him feel that he was letting Ben down.

Ben's frog could croak. His space monster could squelch. And his electronic robot could burble away for hours if its batteries were the right way round.

Even the little toy that Ben called Grey Thing could make a noise, and nobody knew what Grey Thing was meant to be!

Nobody could make Threadbear's squeaker work.

Ben's dad couldn't do it.   His mum couldn't do it.

Nor could his auntie or his grandma.

N̲or could any
of his friends.

When Ben had measles he asked the doctor about Threadbear's squeaker.

The doctor listened to Threadbear's tummy. But there was no squeak. Not even the faintest sign of one.

The other toys tried to help.

'If you had a winder like me, we could wind you up,' said Frog.

'If you were made of rubber like me, we could squelch you,' said the space monster.

'If you had batteries like me, we could turn you on,' said the robot. It was not much help.

'Why don't you ask Father Christmas?' said Grey Thing. 'He knows all about toys.'

This was a brilliant idea and Grey Thing went a little pink.

'But where does Father Christmas live?' asked Threadbear.

'At a place called the North Pole,' said Grey Thing. 'You can get to it up the chimney I think.'

Threadbear had never climbed up a chimney before. It was hard work. He took a wrong turn and fell back down. But he did not give up.

It was long after bedtime when Threadbear poked his head out of the chimney pot.

This must be the North Pole!

Threadbear sat down to wait for Father
Christmas. He waited and waited. But Father
Christmas did not seem to be coming.
The moon rose into the sky and
Threadbear began to doze...

They flew over the top of the world and on
to the land where the squeaker trees grow.

It tasted delicious but it made
Threadbear feel sleepy.

'You must eat the biggest squeaker fruit,'
said Father Christmas.

Threadbear could hear the squeaker
trees as they came in to land.

Threadbear felt himself
falling and falling...

Suddenly Father Christmas was there
helping Threadbear into his sleigh!

Bump! Threadbear woke up. He rubbed his eyes and looked around. There was no squeaker fruit, no squeaker tree and worst of all no Father Christmas.

'I must have fallen asleep and dropped off the North Pole!' said Threadbear.

In the morning Ben was surprised to find Threadbear in the garden covered with soot. Ben's mum put Threadbear straight into the washing machine. She did not even look at the label on Threadbear's neck which read in capital letters DO NOT WASH!

When Threadbear came out of the washing machine the soot was gone, but there was a curious purple stain on his chin, which nobody could explain. Threadbear was feeling too giddy to notice. His head felt like a spinning top!

'I don't mind feeling giddy,' thought
Threadbear as he hung on the line.
'I don't mind having a button for an
eye and a paw that doesn't match.
I don't even mind being hung up by the
ear. But what I DO mind, what I mind
VERY MUCH is having a silly
squeaker in my tummy
that won't SQUEAK!'

Threadbear was so cross that he
frightened a robin. It flew away leaving
him alone in the garden bouncing angry
little bounces on the washing line.

The sun rose slowly over the garden.
It shone straight down on Threadbear,
a great warm shine like an enormous hug.
Threadbear began to steam. He began to
feel better. The more he steamed the
better he felt.

He swung his legs backwards and
forwards. Then he kicked them high in the
air. Soon he was swinging round and round
the washing line giggling to himself.

'Why do I feel so happy?' he wondered.

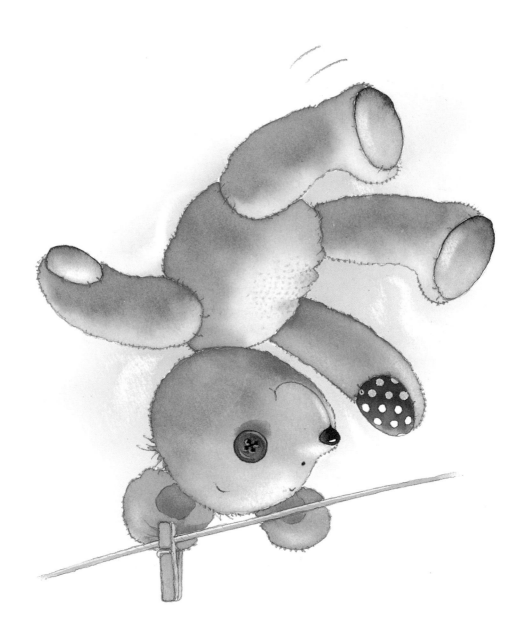

It was at this moment that Threadbear realised a very odd thing had happened to him. His paws felt different. So did his arms and his legs. They were no longer hard!

And inside his tummy was a wonderful, loose, comfortable feeling that he had never felt before!

At the very same moment something caught Threadbear's eye. Something red was racing across the sun. And to Threadbear's surprise the red something was waving goodbye!

When Ben came out to see
if Threadbear was dry he
noticed that his little brown
bear had changed.
'Look mum,' said Ben,
'He's gone floppy!'
Ben's mum unpegged
Threadbear's ear. 'Oh dear!' she said,
'His stuffing must have shrunk in the wash!'
Ben looked at Threadbear. 'I like him
like that. It makes him look...' But Ben
could not think of the right word so instead
he gave Threadbear a squeeze.
And for the first time the squeaker
in Threadbear's tummy gave the
loudest,
clearest,
squeakiest...

. . . squeak!